CW01276758

The Legend of the Brave Soldier

Pentathlon Legend

By Di Pen

Copyright © 2020 by Di Pen

All rights reserved. No part of this book may be used or reproduced in any manner without written permission from the author, except for the use of brief quotations embodied in reviews.

Illustrations by Dejlik Larisa.

For permission requests, write to the publisher, addressed "Attention: Permissions Coordinator," at the address below:

Email: amazukr@gmail.com

ISBN: 9798676075811

Imprint: Independently published

First printing, 2020

Table of Contents

Under siege

- "Our fortress has been under siege for five days. If we do not get any reinforcements, we will be in trouble." - Said General Goodlight, referring to his adjutant Pierre.

- "We must send somebody to get help," the General continued.

- "Who shall we send to break through the enemy camp?"

"An enemy army stands in a ring behind the fortress, then the river with its strong current also has to be crossed.

"Also, there are many other dangers on the way. The wolf is hungry now, and the bear is rambling through the forest.

"I have some well-trained soldiers who could tackle this task. One of them is Gustav, but he is not good when it comes to standing strong in the water," - the General reasoned, pacing around the room. "Nikolai is wounded; he will not make it. Alex has also just recovered after being injured. Peter is not very fast and may not do well in tricky situations. And Philip will be most useful by staying here; he is the best gunner." Said the General.

- "Well, what do you think? Who shall we send?" The General asked his adjutant.

Without hesitation, the adjutant exclaimed,

- "Do not think any longer about this matter, send me!"

The adjutant was a young man, physically well-built. He had already participated in many battles and shown his courage while fighting with enemies.

The General looked intently into his eyes, and asked,

- "Do you think you can handle it?"

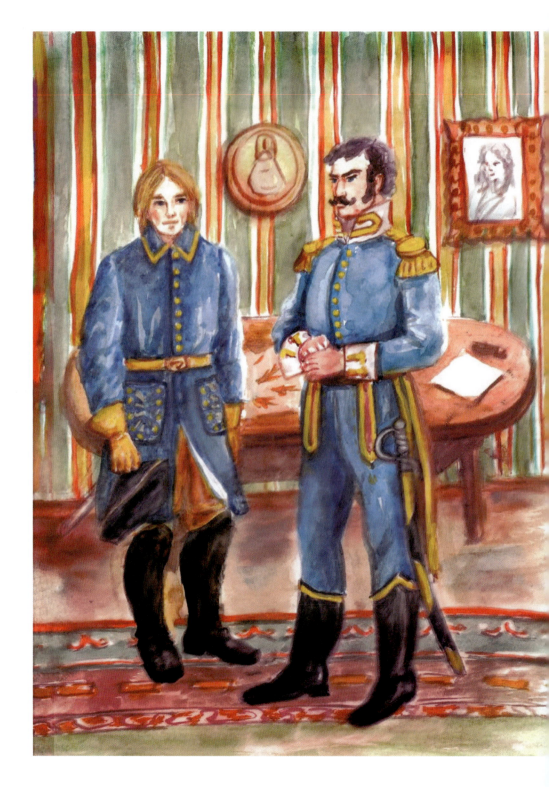

- "Of course, I can handle it!" - the adjutant answered – "I am a good swimmer, I've been sitting in the saddle since I was a child, and I can fight anyone in a battle with swords."

- "Yes, you are a good fencer; you were probably born with a sword in your hands," - the General said with a smile.

- "I saw you in the battle; you are a brave boy and an excellent shooter. You can reload the weapon very quickly. However, we always went to battle as a team; this time, you will need to go alone. No one will help you in difficult times; no one will cover your back. You can rely only on yourself. Moreover, the forest will be challenging to navigate alone!"

- "I can handle it! I grew up in the village near the forest. The forest is my element. I know how to survive there. Many times, I have tracked the beast alone, for three to four days, and always succeeded. You have no reason to doubt my suitability; I am well versed in the terrain, and I am familiar with forest food. As for the wolves and bears, I can smell them from miles away. I will not fall!"

- "Maybe you can do it ..." – thought the General, while scrolling through other options in his head.

Then, he straightened up, looked the adjutant directly in the eyes, and thundered,

- "It is decided! You'll take a letter tomorrow before sunrise! No one should know about your mission, do you hear me? No one. The enemy must not get a whiff of anything.

"Now, go to your room and rest. Come back to me at 3 a.m., and you will receive all your instructions. You are to leave one hour before sunrise. In the meantime, I will try to find a suitable horse, and write a letter."

Pierre went out, and the General began to write a letter to his good friend, Colonel Broome, who was supposed to be staying in a camp for several days, just a one-day journey from the besieged fortress.

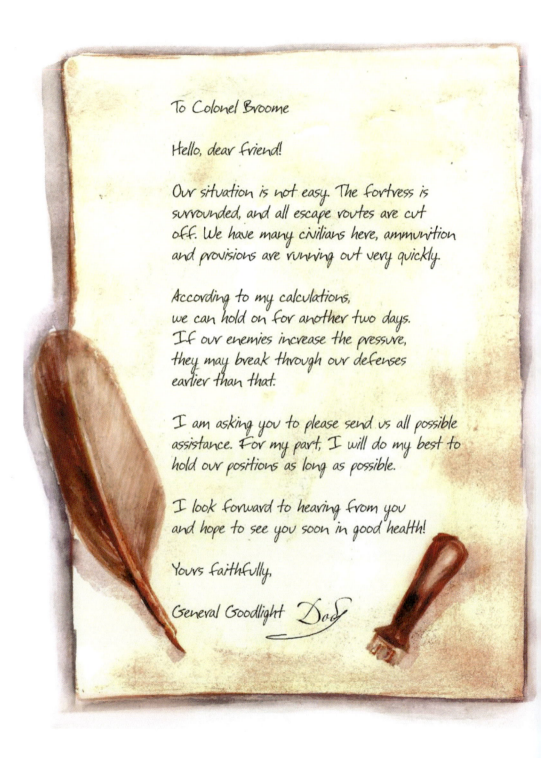

To Colonel Broome

Hello, dear friend!

Our situation is not easy. The fortress is
surrounded, and all escape routes are cut
off. We have many civilians here, ammunition
and provisions are running out very quickly.

According to my calculations,
we can hold on for another two days.
If our enemies increase the pressure,
they may break through our defenses
earlier than that.

I am asking you to please send us all possible
assistance. For my part, I will do my best to
hold our positions as long as possible.

I look forward to hearing from you
and hope to see you soon in good health!

Yours faithfully,

General Goodlight

Letter to Colonel Broome

Hello, dear friend!

Our situation is not easy. The fortress is surrounded, and all escape routes are cut off.

We have many civilians here, ammunition and provisions are running out very quickly.

According to my calculations, we can hold on for another two days. If our enemies increase the pressure, they may break through our defenses earlier than that.

I am asking you to please send us all possible assistance. For my part, I will do my best to hold our positions as long as possible.

I look forward to hearing from you and hope to see you soon in good health!

Yours faithfully,

General Goodlight

The General folded the letter, sealed it in a special waterproof envelope, put his own stamp on it, and hid it in the inside pocket of his uniform.

Horse selection

On leaving his headquarters, the General went directly to the stable, where he hoped to find at least some horses.

On arriving there, he saw a stableman and two skinny horses. One of them was well cleaned and looked much better than the

second, which was dirty, with old abrasions and scars on her skin.

The stalls for the horses were nothing special, but they were so clean that even insects could find no peace there.

- "Good afternoon," the General greeted the stableman.

- "Good afternoon," the groom replied.

- "Are these all the remaining horses?"

- "Yes, only these two are left."

- "The choice is not great. Which one is better?" asked the General

- This one, of course," said the groom, pointing at the well-cleaned horse.

- "Well then, do not feed or give drink to the second nag. Food and water are running out, and we need to preserve it." The General said and pretended to leave.

The groom's eyes almost popped out of their sockets! He quickly ran to the General, fell to his knees, and said with tears in his eyes:

- "Your Honor, forgive me. Do not ruin the horse; it is dirty and has old scars, but it is the best horse in the area! I specifically kept her looking this way so that nobody would take and ruin her!"

- "What do you think that I don't understand which one is the good horse, and which is the nag?" The General replied with a smile.

"I realized immediately that this dirty horse is not a nag, but a fire-horse! The scars on her skin are from fighting, not from hard work. And she behaves much more calmly at the sight of my combat uniform than the other horse. It is clear that this 'dirty' horse is smart and has been in combat many times.

"Get the horses saddled, drink and feed them, make sure they are prepared and then take them to my headquarters. Do not save water and food; let them drink and eat plenty. We need to distribute equipment and provisions to the soldiers early in the morning."

The groom nodded affirmatively and wiped his eyes as he began to comply with the General's order.

Adjutant

On his way home, Pierre was thinking about the upcoming adventure. His head was spinning. What do I wear? What do I take with me?

He decided that he would take a small supply of provisions and some water.

He would wear boots with gaiters*, hiking pants, a shirt, a tunic, and a hat. For the weapon, he would take a pistol, cartridges, a sword, and a knife.

- "Anything else will only slow me down," thought the adjutant.

Arriving home, he dined modestly on dried crackers and a handful of nuts mixed with dried fruits and washed it all down with water.

After that, Pierre decided to sleep and have a good rest before the upcoming trip. But the excitement and anticipation of the upcoming journey kept him awake. So, he lay for about two hours with his eyes closed; at midnight, he finally fell asleep.

* *Gaiters - special leather pads worn on the shin which protect the rider from chafing when riding a horse.*

The General

On his return to headquarters, the General began to study the map of the upcoming route. The path for the young adjutant was not an easy one:

- He must leave the fortress very quietly.
- Break through the enemy camp on horseback.
- Ride through the prairie.
- Overcome the dense forest.
- Cross the strong river.
- Go through another forest and, without getting lost, get to Colonel Broome's camp and put the letter directly into his hands.

- "This dangerous trip should take less than a day, but let's see how it goes," the General thought to himself.

Having drawn the path for the adjutant on the map, the General folded it and put the map in his uniform pocket, together with the prepared letter. Then he went outside to check the horses that had just been brought.

It was already dark. The General checked the horses and saddles holding his torchlight. Everything was good.

The groom stood nearby and waited for further instructions.

- "We'll let you know when we have sorted everything out, but for now, go home, we don't need any interference here," the General said.

The groom expected to stay with the horses, but the General's tone showed him that asking to do so was useless. The groom stroked the horses and wandered home.

The beginning of the campaign

At the agreed time, the adjutant arrived and saw that two horses were standing near the headquarters entrance. He was a little surprised: "Is anyone else going with me?" He thought and knocked on the door.

After a few seconds, the General opened the door and immediately led Pierre to the table, where he turned the map around and showed the adjutant the detailed plan for the upcoming trip.

After instructing the adjutant, the General told him why the second horse was needed. Nobody was going with Pierre, but the second horse would serve as a decoy for the enemy!

- "Do you have any questions?" The General asked Pierre.

- "No, everything is clear!" answered the adjutant.

- "Excellent. As you see, an exciting adventure awaits you. Don't hesitate. I want to hunt wild pheasants as soon as possible," the General said with a smile. Then he folded up the map and, taking out the envelope with the letter, handed them to the young adjutant.

- "Well, good luck!"

Pierre carefully folded both bundles and put them in the secret pocket of his trousers, which was behind his belt.

Leaving the house, they took a horse each and walked towards the fortress gate. As they approached the gate, the General again looked at Pierre and checked his weapons and clothes — everything was in order.

– "Sit on your horse, and lead the second horse with you on a leash, as was agreed."

Slapping Pierre on the shoulder, he added:

- "I believe in you. You will succeed! Do what you can, listen to your heart, and avoid unnecessary risks. Our lives are in your hands!"

Pierre thanked the General, firmly shaking his hand, mounted the scarred horse, tied a rope holding the second horse to his saddle, and headed to the gate.

The guard began to open the gate, and by order of the General, they put out the torches, so the enemy would not suspect something was wrong.

The gates opened quickly, and Pierre, without turning back, quietly left the fortress.

After a few seconds, the General could no longer see the silhouette of the adjutant. Pierre had disappeared into the dark.

Meeting with the enemy

After the gates had closed behind him, Pierre moved towards the enemy fires. He had learned the route map very well, but, like the General, he did not exactly know where the enemy sentinels were or where the torches glowed.

According to scouts, the sentinels were not very close to each other. Usually, they stood in a clearly visible area, so he decided to move along a small lowland. Darkness made it possible to get closer to the enemy camp, evaluate its location, and choose the safest way to break through the enemy ring.

Everything went according to plan. Pierre almost reached the enemy encampment and was about to bypass one of the luminous torches on the right side, when he suddenly heard the scream: "Stop! Who goes there?"

Pierre knew that it would not be easy to see a rider from the lighted place the guards were in. Probably the sentinels had heard the sound from the horse hooves.

Pierre quietly untied the rope with the second horse from his saddle and pushed it straight into the enemy light. She immediately ran to the torches, probably hoping to get some food.

"The General is an excellent strategist," thought the young adjutant as he spurred his horse, rushed forward, and went around the sentinels on the left side.

Shots were heard. Pierre realized that they were not shooting at him, but at the horse, which he had let go. After three shots, the shooting stopped. So far, everything was going well thought the adjutant as he rode into the enemy camp at full speed. But, at that very moment, from both his left and right, he saw several people running out of tents, and five more running towards him. Apparently, all of them had jumped out because of the noise of shots.

Pierre spurred his horse even harder, and rushed forward with a thunderous speed, right towards five soldiers.

They barely managed to bounce to the side when they saw Pierre riding down on them. As the wind of his passing swept between the enemy soldiers, without turning to either side, he continued his race through the enemy camp.

Lights were lit on both sides, and more and more soldiers appeared every second. Pierre caught the enemy by surprise; they did not have time to do anything to stop the rider who was racing at full speed, jumping over barrels, benches, and tables that were in his way.

Chase

Finally, Pierre broke through the enemy's ring, and without slowing down his gallop, he directed his horse towards the forest.

The sun started to rise, and the adjutant could see that there were only a few miles left before he would reach the forest. Suddenly, Pierre heard shots behind him! A few bullets passed very closely.

The adjutant turned around and saw a horse detachment of the enemy, which had set off after him in pursuit. They had realized that Pierre was a messenger who was going for help, so a group was sent to stop him.

The shots began to increase, and Pierre felt that his horse's pace had slowed.

There was very little distance left to the forest when, after the next shot, his horse squealed, beat its hind hooves, and fell down on the ground.

Pierre successfully jumped from the horse to avoid being crushed on the ground. Turning back, he saw that the enemies were approaching very quickly, but the forest was also nearby.

At the same time, several enemy riders, who had pulled ahead of the rest of the group of pursuers, quickly began to overtake the adjutant.

Hearing the approaching clatter of hooves, Pierre, without hesitation, took out a pistol, turned back, and, taking aim, took five shots at the pursuing riders.

With the first and second shots, he hit the horse of the closest enemy. It stopped immediately, fell to the ground, and crushed its rider on the ground.

The remaining shots injured and threw the second soldier to the ground while his horse, without stopping, continued to race straight at Pierre.

Pierre threw off the tunic that was hindering him, gathered all his forces, and ran in the same direction as the horse of the downed rider. When the adjutant caught up with the enemy horse, he grabbed the stirrup* with his hand and, barely staying on his feet, pulled himself up and climbed onto the horse

A minute later, Pierre was in the wood! He quickly stopped the horse, jumped from it, and ran deep into the forest. It was better to move on without a horse because the enemy could easily follow the horse's tracks, and the branches of trees and bushes were very thick.

The forest was salvation for Pierre.

In the wood

Having jumped over a tall bush, Pierre abruptly changed direction and rushed on.

"They definitely can't catch me in here!" thought Pierre, as he kept running quickly through the forest. But his joy did not last long. After a few minutes, he heard dogs barking behind him! This was a complete surprise for the young adjutant. Most likely, the second unit was sent to search for the first, with the dogs.

Dogs could easily track Pierre, especially since they had accurately sniffed his first horse, and used it as scent. By listening to the barking, it was possible to determine that the distance of the pursuers was about two miles, but it was gradually decreasing.

Stirrup - part of the saddle into which the rider's foot is inserted.

Pierre remembered his grandfather, who told him how to hide his smell on the hunt so that the beast wouldn't be able to smell a person. The adjutant plucked several coniferous branches and rubbed them well onto his boots and gaiters. Then he crumpled the needles with the mixed leaves of the bushes and rubbed his body and clothes with hem. Maybe this would help put the dogs off the track?

Having run a few more miles, Pierre felt a strong sense of hunger. The last time he ate had been in the morning, before leaving the fortress, and since then, a lot of time had passed.

Pierre could not afford to stop to eat and relax; he could still hear the dogs barking behind him. As he ran, he ate a handful of dried fruit and some nuts. Having washed it all down with water, the young adjutant felt much better.

Running through the forest was difficult. Fallen trees, impenetrable thickets, and low tree branches sometimes greatly slowed the pace of the soldier. But his pursuers also faced the same difficulties. Therefore, the distance between them closed very slowly.

Pierre was well oriented in the forest and knew exactly which direction in which to move. The sun and moss on the trees perfectly showed the cardinal directions. The course lay north.

River

The chase lasted a long time. According to Pierre's calculations, the river must be close. People from the fortress said that the current in it was strong and treacherous, with many whirlpools. Therefore, you needed to know exactly where and how to cross the river.

There was a bridge, but it was risky to cross it; for sure, it had already been destroyed, or there could be an ambush.

About an hour later, Pierre noticed that there was more greenery in the forest, and after a few minutes, he had heard the sound of water.

"The river is close!" Pierre thought and enthusiastically rushed in its direction.

The barking of the dogs began to be heard more clearly; the rubbing of needles and leaves had not helped. The distance from the pursuers was reduced to a minimum. The young adjutant could already hear the voices of the people led by the dogs.

Pierre went through a large bush, and his eyes opened onto a beautiful view of the river. Along its banks were scattered stone blocks and a lot of prickly bushes and reeds. The river was approximately two hundred meters wide. The rapid current, with whirlpools near the shore, made the river very dangerous. Only a well-trained swimmer could deal with such an element.

To cross the river, it was necessary to bypass the whirlpools, overcome the current, and get to the other side at a suitable place. Otherwise, the river could catch you and hit you with the stones, and even worse, you could get into the whirlpool and drown there. All these thoughts revolved in Pierre's head as he ran along the coast, jumping from stone to stone, looking for a suitable place to cross the river.

Very soon, two dogs appeared from the forest, with pursuers running after them. They immediately noticed the adjutant and, without slowing down, rushed to catch up with him.

Finally, Pierre saw a suitable place where it was possible to cross the river. But, in order to get to it, it was necessary to go around the dense thickets of a tall shrub, climb onto a ledge of a cliff, jump over a whirlpool, and dive into the river.

Pierre had almost run into the bush when he heard a series of shots in his direction.

He immediately ducked down and hid behind a nearby large stone, which was good protection from the enemy's bullets. The adjutant took out his pistol and fired several shots in response, noticeably stopping the pursuers.

The shootout started. Enemy soldiers also took refuge behind stones scattered on the shore and began to rush in order to get close to the adjutant.

The cartridges were running out, and the enemies were getting closer and closer. Pierre noticed how several soldiers hid in the forest. They probably meant to go around the adjutant and come from the rear.

"You can't delay; you need to act!" thought Pierre.

Continuing to shoot at his opponents and hide behind the stones, the adjutant, with rapid dashes, began to move towards the large rock. Having wounded several enemies, he heard the idle click of his gun. He was out of bullets.

Pierre threw the gun to the ground, went around the bush, ran to the ledge of the rock, and pushing off with one foot, jumped as far as possible into the watery abyss!

The enemies noticed Pierre's daring move, realized that they would not be there in time to catch him and let the dogs go.

One of the dogs ran to the cliff and rushed after the adjutant, but it failed to jump over the whirlpool, landing right in it.

The second dog did not dare to take the dangerous jump. She remained still and kept barking on the rock. The enemy soldiers arrived a minute later.

Three daredevils quickly dropped their equipment and, leaving only one sword, jumped after Pierre into the water. The rest remained on the rock, periodically firing in the adjutant's direction, but their bullets flew past him.

Emerging from the water, Pierre overcame the strong current and, with all his energy, swam to the opposite shore, to a place where it was safe to get out of the water.

Soon, the shots from the rock fell silent. One of the enemy soldiers began to catch up with Pierre! Seeing this, the enemy soldiers joyfully began to scream and wave their hands, supporting their comrade.

Fight on the shore

There was quite a bit of coastline. Pierre tried to run, but he had already exhausted his strength. His hands were numb, his sword pulled his body down, and he couldn't breathe enough air.

After a few more strokes, Pierre touched the bottom with his hands.

– "I did it!" The adjutant was delighted and quickly stood up to leave the water. Suddenly, he heard splashes behind him. Turning around, he saw that a soldier had almost overtaken him!

Two more enemies were at a considerable distance behind. They were being carried down by the river; apparently, they were swimming worse than their companion.

A moment later, the enemy soldier was next to the adjutant and taking out his sword.

The adjutant was ready for it; taking a few steps back, he quickly drew his sword and repelled the first attack of the enemy.

A battle ensued. The fighters attacked each other in turn, lunging and trying to inflict injury on an arm or leg, occasionally trying to hit their opponent's chest.

After several attacks, the fighters' strength began to fade.

Pierre noticed that the two soldiers who were behind had almost crossed the river, and they would soon come ashore. It would be very difficult for him to fight with three opponents.

Gathering all his strength, Pierre went on the attack. He barely hit the enemy's blade with the edge of his sword, and making a long attack forward, he pricked him in the chest. The enemy dropped the sword from his hands, staggered, and fell into the river, which caught and carried him downstream.

At the same moment, the other two soldiers came close to the shore and, seeing what had happened to their comrade, wanted to attack Pierre immediately.

But the savvy adjutant started picking stones up from the bottom of the river and threw them at his opponents. The soldiers were shoulder-deep in the water, so they could not quickly get close to Pierre, and they tried to beat off the flying stones with their hands.

Then one of the soldiers noticed that his sword was gone; most likely, he had dropped it as he had fought the strong current of the river.

He paused for breath to decide what to do next. At the same moment, a stone thrown by Pierre fell directly on his forehead, after which he dropped to his knees and went underwater.

Without wasting time, Pierre ran ashore and turned to his opponent, prepared to repel another attack.

The enemy who came out of the water was firmly built and very tall, taller than the adjutant!

The furious soldier rushed at the adjutant, shouting words in a strange language. Pierre immediately realized that the enemy was a skilled fencer. He knew this by how well the fighter worked with the blade of his sword and how he moved and kept his distance in battle. Pierre worked hard to repulse the giant's first attack.

At the same time, the enemy did not expect that he would receive such a rebuff from the young adjutant; he defended himself well and periodically counterattacked. This tactic of the battle forced the giant

to move quickly, and exert more effort, which led to a loss of his strength.

The fight dragged on. Both swordsmen were pretty tired. They hardly held the swords in their hands, and their movements became slower every second.

All this time, a detachment of the remaining soldiers were on the opposite shore, watching what was happening from the cliff. Fortunately for Pierre, they did not jump into the water. Most likely due to because they were not good swimmers.

A few minutes later, the weary giant tried to attack the adjutant again but, not having time to quickly step back, missed Pierre's counterattack, which struck the giant's chest with the lightning-fast movement of his blade. The giant staggered and fell into the water.

The battle was over.

Exhausted, Pierre lowered his sword, looked at the opposite bank where enemy soldiers stood silently on the rock, and turned and headed for the dense thickets of forest.

On the road again

The chase was over. The firm determination to reach the allied camp as quickly as possible meant the exhausted Pierre could not relax. There was no time for rest.

Pierre checked the letter, and fortunately, it was in place. Then, he pulled the remaining mixture of nuts and dried berries out of his pocket, which had been soaked in the river's water. He ate

them and set off on the road. As he ran past the stream, he drank mouthfuls of spring water, and immediately felt a surge of strength.

Having looked at the position of the setting sun, the adjutant determined the direction of the path and ran at full speed towards the supposed site of the allied camp.

Pierre made his way through the dense thicket of the forest, sometimes jumping over dry logs and small ditches on the ground, while constantly scratching against thorns, bushes, and other undergrowth.

It got dark outside, and the silhouettes of trees began to merge, but Pierre did not stop; he kept running forward. He couldn't see anything, and different thoughts began to spin in his head, "Have I lost my way?" "Maybe it's worth having a little rest?" The adjutant quickly drove these thoughts away from himself and, without slowing down, continued to run through the forest even faster.

Allied camp

After running a little further, Pierre noticed that the forest had thinned; there were fewer trees and bushes.

Suddenly, in the distance, he saw a light. Pierre rushed forward with all his strength. He was about three kilometers away from the lights!

Running closer, he realized that the lights were torches that surrounded the soldiers' camp. Sneaking closer, the adjutant was finally able to discern a drawing on a swinging banner - it was an allied camp!

The camp was situated in an open area and stood on a small elevation, which made it inconvenient for an enemy attack.

Getting close to the camp, the adjutant raised his hands up and shouted:

- "Do not shoot. I am not an enemy" and moved to the sentries.

A moment later, two armed soldiers stopped Pierre.

- "I have an important message for your commander," Pierre said to the sentries.

- "Tell him immediately that it is from General Goodlight!"

The sentries looked at each other.

- "What are you waiting for? Hurry up! We can't spare a minute!" Pierre shouted menacingly.

- "We will notify him as soon as you hand over your weapon! No one can be trusted now," said one of the sentries.

Pierre gave his sword to sentries. At the same time, four more soldiers from the camp approached.

One of them once again asked Pierre about the purpose of his visit and said that he could transmit the letter himself.

- "I must personally convey the message from the General," Pierre answered him.

- "Well then, I hope you have a really important message. If not, then you will get in trouble!" the soldier who had just arrived said coldly. Apparently, he was a senior guard.

The two sentries remained in their place, and the rest of the soldiers surrounded Pierre and led him to a large tent located in the middle of the camp. This was the headquarters of the Colonel.

Colonel

When the soldiers approached the tent, one of the soldiers accompanying Pierre informed the guard about the guest. The guard went into the tent, and a minute later came out, inviting the young adjutant and the soldiers accompanying him to enter.

Entering the tent, Pierre was blinded by a bright light emanating from several lighted lamps, which made his eyes close tightly. After a few seconds, he saw the commander, who was delighted!

An interesting picture was in front of the Colonel's eyes. A young man stood in front of him with a tattered face, covered in abrasions and cuts, in worn-out boots, but with kind blue eyes and a wide smile. The General was amazed at what he saw but, remaining detached, asked:

- "Good evening. What urgency has brought you to us at such a late hour, young man?"

- "I have a letter for you. I was ordered to hand it to you in person," Pierre stated, and, taking out a thick envelope from his inner pocket, handed it to the Colonel.

The Colonel took the envelope, opened it and, having read the letter, asked Pierre:

- "How is General Goodlight doing? Still, loves to hunt rabbits?"

- "The General is in good health, but he loves hunting pheasants!" answered Pierre.

And then Pierre understood why the General had told him about the hunt before leaving. It was a secret code between old friends! Only in this way could the Colonel believe that he was facing a

real messenger, not a spy who could force the allied troops into a trap! Hearing the adjutant's response, the Colonel said in a thunderous voice:

- "We are leaving camp! Moving south!"

The Colonel went up to Pierre, shook his hand and, looking directly into his eyes, said:

- "Courage is the best decoration for man. Thank you!"

***

The General was in his headquarters when he heard a knock on the door.

- "Come in?" the General said.

A guard from the walls of the fortress entered and quickly exclaimed:

- "General, you need to see this! The enemy is rushing to lift the siege and leave! We do not understand what has happened!"

The General smiled and said in reply to the soldier:

- "Ah Pierre, brave Pierre. Well done!"

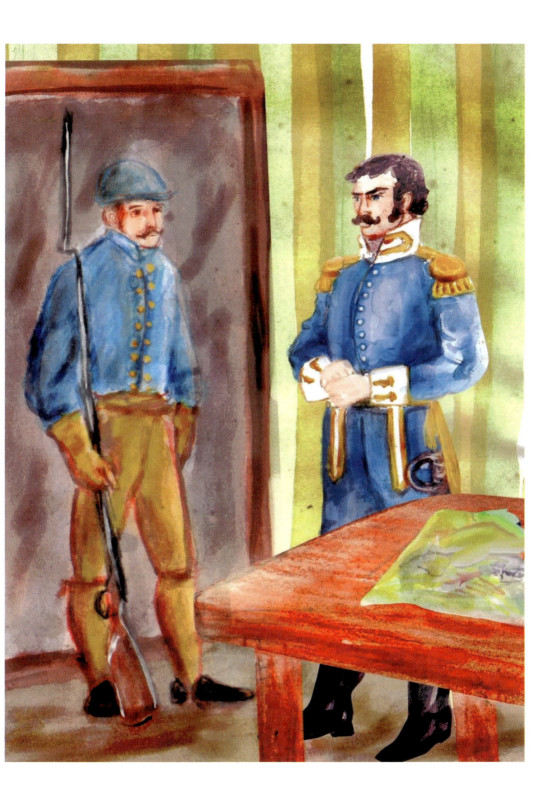

Epilogue

The siege was lifted very fast! When the enemies heard of the approach of reinforcements, they decided not to engage in a battle; the risk of being pinched between the two allies was very high.

Colonel Broome arrived with his troops in time and met his fighting friend in good health.

The happy General gathered the whole army together and thanked the young adjutant. Finally saying:

- "Thank you, Pierre. You have not only saved your comrades from trouble, but you also passed a serious life test, and you became a real Officer!"

The General's words were the best reward for Pierre!

Afterword

Subsequently, this story about Pierre became a legend, which clearly shows the qualities every person should have, namely courage, determination, and self-discipline. All these qualities are inherent in modern pentathlon athletes.

The modern pentathlon is an Olympic sport that includes the five disciplines described in this book: horse riding, running, shooting, swimming, and fencing.

All of them harmoniously develop the personality and strengthen the spirit and body of a person.

Get involved in sports!

Printed in Great Britain
by Amazon

72131944R00026